T0161252

SILENCE DESCENDS

SILENCE DESCENDS

The End of the Information Age
2000–2500

GEORGE CASE

ARSENAL PULP PRESS
Vancouver

To T.G.

SILENCE DESCENDS

Copyright © 1997 by George Case

ARSENAL PULP PRESS
103–1014 Homer Street
Vancouver, B.C.
Canada v6b 2w9

The publisher gratefully acknowledges the support of the Canada Council for the Arts for its publishing program, and the support of the Book Publishing Industry Development Program and the B.C. Arts Council.

Typeset by the Vancouver Desktop Publishing Centre
Photographs by Rosalee Hiebert
Printed and bound in Canada by Webcom

CANADIAN CATALOGUING IN PUBLICATION DATA
Case, George, 1967–
  Silence descends

  ISBN 1-55152-041-9

  I. Title.
PS855.A7739S54 1997   C813'.54   C97-9710172-7
PR9199.3.C4285S54 1997

. . . For a multitude of causes, unknown to former times, are now acting with a combined force to blunt the discriminating powers of the mind, and, unfitting it for all voluntary exertion, to reduce it to a state of almost savage torpor. The most effective of these causes are the great national events which are daily taking place, and the increasing accumulation of men in cities, where the uniformity of their occupations produces a craving for extraordinary incident, which the rapid communication of intelligence hourly gratifies. To this tendency of life and manners the literature and theatrical exhibitions of the country have conformed themselves. . . . When I think upon this degrading thirst after outrageous stimulation, I am almost ashamed to have spoken of the feeble endeavour made in these volumes to counteract it; and, reflecting upon the magnitude of the general evil, I should be oppressed with no dishonourable melancholy, had I not a deep impression of certain inherent and indestructible qualities of the human mind, and likewise of certain powers in the great and permanent objects that act upon it, which are equally inherent and indestructible; and were there not added to this impression a belief, that the time is approaching when the evil will be systematically opposed, by men of greater powers, and with far more distinguished success. . . .

—William Wordsworth,
Preface to the *Lyrical Ballads*, 1800

Introduction

Half a millennium ago, the existence of this book—of *any* book—in the present era would have been barely conceivable. The printed word was thought to be fading into obsolescence, and it was popularly imagined that civilization was entering a new phase where dialogue and discourse would be facilitated by wondrous technologies whose power surpassed that of mere writing as obviously as writing had once outdated cave paintings. Half a millennium ago, men and women saw themselves poised to reap the fullest benefits of what they called "Information," an awesome god whose ever-expanding electronic embrace at last could reach into every home, fulfill every need, save every soul. Half a millennium ago, the world hailed the long-awaited arrival of "The Information Age"; the world did not know that the epoch was already at its zenith, nor that the history of its long, difficult collapse would one day be conveyed with paper, ink, and a medium far more potent than any then envisioned.

Here at the end of the twenty-fifth century, to be sure, there will be those who argue that no decline or fall has taken place.

After all, society still uses the inventions that began the period. Readers will wonder how it can be decreed that the period has now ended. Do we not continue to live with the same tools of mass, instantaneous communication—far more advanced ones, at that—that were around five hundred years ago? What exactly has changed? No living person has a fully accurate answer, but we will attempt to briefly outline the differences between our own culture and that of 2000; the account offered here is intended as a broad overview for the layman, not a detailed study for the specialist. Even broadly speaking, though, we may say a great deal has indeed changed. The title of this work was not chosen recklessly: it is the story of nothing less than revolution and metamorphosis on a global scale.

Much of what contributed to the decline was wholly unanticipated by the citizens who experienced it, but note that some warnings had been sounded far in advance. It would be a gross calumny to portray the populations who lived and died during the Information Age as anything but self-aware: both prominent thinkers and average people alike had often lamented the saturation of their lives with trivial, demeaning, and baldly untrue "enlightenment" whose ceaseless production and consumption seemed an inherent vice of their social systems. "Information," they said, was really a deformed child of industrialism, exploiting rather than enhancing human intelligence, turning thought and feeling into commodities to be bought and sold, reducing the mind to a marketplace. In 1961 Newton Minow, Chairman of the American Federal Communications Commission, famously described television (then in its infancy) as "a vast wasteland"; the novelists Aldous Huxley, in *Brave New World* (1932), and George Orwell, in *Nineteen Eighty-Four* (1949), had alerted wide audiences to their capacity to be distracted by shallow entertainments at the expense of their political autonomy; transcendentalist philosopher Henry Thoreau (1817–1862) inspired millions with his literate rebukes of base commercialism and urban alienation; and as early as the dawn of the Industrial Revolution in the eighteenth century, the Romantic writers, such as William Blake (1757–1827), William Wordsworth (1770–1850), and John Keats (1795–1821), mourned the growing pre-eminence of cold reason, rationalism, and intellect over feeling, spirituality, and intuition. Yet these and numerous other observers, influential though they were, had failed to prevent the inexorable rise of the Information Age. They must have cursed their prescience as much as we admire it. Fortunately, perhaps, they never lived to see the waking manifestations of their worst nightmares.

Those who *did* endure the most claustrophobic years of so-called "data glut" could do little but resign themselves to it. Others had seen it coming; no one dared believe it would end. We know today, of course, that what ultimately (and quite literally) shattered the foundations of the Information Age was beyond prediction, but even its harshest critics at the time expressed only stymied dismay, a sort of philosophical shaking of heads. The voices of protest were meek and pessimistic. It was not until the earliest crises of the new millennium had occurred that people warily, hesitantly began to picture an eventual close to the historical chapter they had been living in. The most familiar of these figures to us is Katsuichi Yamashiro (1990–2043), the Japanese poet and engineer whose haiku is still recalled:

> At last the wind dies
> Now a stillness calms the trees
> Now silence descends

The Information Age is no more. Our world is engaged with a new and different reality than the one it has known for many generations; we no longer live in a constant, clamorous disorder. Human activity has advanced past ancient dichotomies of physical and metaphysical, material and immaterial, flesh and spirit. The affairs of our species are conducted in an unprecedented quiet. It has been nearly five hundred years since the voice of the planet began to fall to the deep whisper that we listen for today, since the Information god first faltered, since that late summer's day when the first vast hush came down, terrible and pristine.

"I keep figuring how it will be." She spoke very softly, to a point just past him on the wall. "Somehow I think of the churches as going first, before even the Empire State Building. And then all the big apartment houses by the river, slipping down slowly into the water with the people inside. And the schools, in the middle of Latin class maybe, while we're reading Caesar." She brought her eyes to his face, looking at him in numb excitement. . . .

"The office buildings will be just piles of broken stones," she said, her wide emphatic eyes still looking at him. "If only you could know exactly what *minute* it will come. . . .

"Things will be different afterward," she said. "Everything that makes the world like it is now will be gone. We'll have new rules and new ways of living. Maybe there'll be a law not to live in houses, so then no one can hide from anyone else, you see. . . ."

"Well," he said, with a little laugh. "You make it sound very interesting. Sorry I won't be there to see it." He stopped, his shoulder against the swinging door into the dining-room. He wanted badly to say something adult and scathing, and yet he was afraid of showing her that he had listened to her, that when he was young people had not talked like that.

—Shirley Jackson, "The Intoxicated," 1949

CHAPTER ONE

"May You Live In Interesting Times"

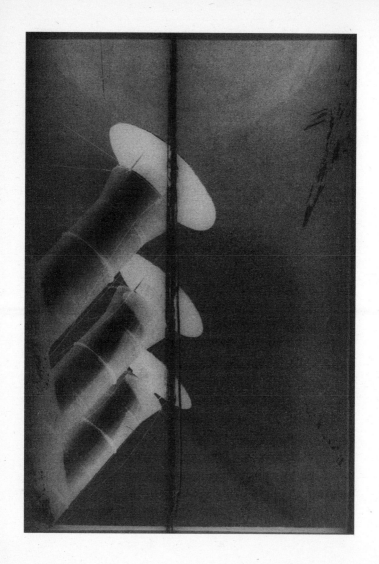

In 2004 the city of Volgograd, Russia, had just begun to link up with the burgeoning networks of information banks, databases, and intercommunication systems that were then crisscrossing the earth. Its 1.1 million inhabitants, like most of their countrymen, were still trying to cope with an economy crippled by stubborn, doddering bureaucracies, meager harvests, and the fluctuating feasts and famines of international trade; however dazzling the powers of sophisticated technology may have been, they remained largely inaccessible to all but a handful of academics, scientists, entrepreneurs, and government officials.

Yet people in Volgograd were not isolated—the expensive consumer products necessary for manipulating digital intelligence were financially out of range for most of them, but radios, televisions, videotapes and videotape players, telephones, audio tapes and discs, motion pictures, photographs, books, magazines, and newspapers were not. Theoretically they lagged behind their wealthier cousins in other cities, but practically they were as within reach of news and ideas as virtually every other man and woman anywhere. Conversely, Volgograd's populace could speak to distant towns, nations or continents via the arsenal of transmitters, cables, and satellite dishes at their disposal—as with any civilized point then on the map, the metropolis broadcast information outward as well as received it, connecting itself in an infinite variety of ways with the infinite other broadcasters and receivers that spanned the globe.

What information Volgograd relayed to its neighbours and to the world was not that different from the material beamed or wired from most Russian communities: news, entertainment, sports coverage, law enforcement records, medical statistics, government directives, weather reports, and all the minutiae of daily life among a struggling but ever-resilient people. The city was distinguished, in 2004, for being the home of football sensation Sergei Titov; as the site of one of the most visible food riots during the infamous "Hungry Winter" of 2001–2002; and historians and a shrinking number of octogenarian veterans recalled an earlier Volgograd, once called Stalingrad, that had been a significant battleground during the Second World War of 1939–1945. Imposing concrete memorials to Stalingrad's defenders stood throughout Volgograd—the towering statue of the Motherland was a much-recognized landmark that still attracted military buffs and tourists. Such was the image of itself—sturdy, striving, and heroically goal-scoring—Volgograd projected to the audience of humanity.

Then, on August 18, 2004, at 1:32 p.m. local time, Volgograd suddenly stopped projecting anything at all. A minute passed; technical crews, systems monitors, and interrupted television viewers in surrounding centres speculated about a power failure at one of Volgograd's enormous hydro-electric stations; no communication broke the puzzling silence. Only when scattered accounts from a wide radius of witnesses began to filter in—from the Caspian Sea, from Stavropol, Rostov, and Astrakhan—did a horrifying explanation present itself: a giant cloud of smoke and flame, shaped like a grotesque, instantly familiar mushroom, was rising up from the Yerengi Hills on the lower Volga River. Within seconds, the story was sent to Europe, the Americas, Africa, Asia, and Oceania. The major Russian city of Volgograd, with a population of over one million men, women, and children, had been devastated by a nuclear bomb.

The atomic levelling of Volgograd can be cited, from our perspective, as the beginning of the end of the Information Age. In 2004 the tragedy was seen as a hideous epilogue to the Cold War of 1945–1990—though never fully confirmed, Russian fascist militants were suspected to have triggered the detonation, the ultimate act of lawlessness in a land whose internal order had dissolved with the fall of its socialist dictatorship fourteen years previously—but today it represents something different. Horrific and completely unexpected, the Volgograd bombing seemed to incapacitate the very means by which people first learned of it; the sheer scale of such an event, the number of human beings killed instantly (over 500, 000), and the manner in which they died (the first direct casualties of nuclear weapons in almost sixty years), seemed profaned in their conveyance by technological methods. News of major incidents had always been delivered as "Information," to be sure, yet here was an incident so awful, so stunning, that no amount of televised images or sounds could do it justice.

It was, as Mary Xian wrote in her *Night Thoughts* (2012), "past all format, defiant of encapsulation, unframeable, irreducible." For the first time, the airwaves of the world had been struck dumb.

But the world carried on. Volgograd was a single episode, an ominous sobering pause; basic social structures and the extensiveness of long-distance data sending had not really been disturbed. Computer networks meshed ever more densely, and their human vassals fell increasingly under their yoke. By 2006 entire geographical regions had become united under sprawling umbrellas of Information: the deafening concentration of commerce and culture electronically ricocheting to and fro in a given area gave rise to terms like "cyberopolis" and "silicon state." One such province was the northeastern seaboard of the United States of America, extending between the cities of Portland, Maine, and Richmond, Virginia, and especially clustered around New York City and the capital city of Washington. A transatlantic equivalent was found in the northwest corner of Europe, where London, Paris, Brussels, Amsterdam, and the Ruhr had grown into a techno-urban jungle, with incomprehensible torrents of trade, management, learning, and recreation being circuited among close to a hundred million people at the speed of light.

Teeming megalopolises such as these were troubled, in the fall of 2006, by a freak heat wave that scorched much of the northern hemisphere. Meteorologists scrambled to diagnose the phenomena as the result of environmental upheavals—"global warming," a volcanic eruption in Chile, the lingering pall of ash from Volgograd—but no hypothesis was convincing and none ultimately mattered. As many hundreds of the most vulnerable citizens (such as the elderly and the ill) succumbed to the heat, their neighbours soaked up power to operate their cooling appliances and to feed their hunger for transmitted knowledge: the networks, they reminded one another, could not be neglected. But on "Dark Friday," September 15, the demand for electricity suddenly surged past the supply, and almost simultaneously the two largest silicon states of two continents were struck by a power failure of unheard-of dimensions.

Dramatic derailings of electrical current were hardly unknown in the early twenty-first century—"blackouts," and the less spectacular "brownouts," had occurred at intervals for several decades, often during periods of extreme weather conditions—but a disparate, synchronous *pair* of crashes was completely, frighteningly new. At 6:15 p.m., Parisian time, and 12:04 p.m. in New York, the synthetic glows and hums of a billion instruments flickered and went out. Backup or "fail-safe" measures were implemented to hold off the chaos, but at first they brought only halting, sporadic respite. Another Volgogradian security breach was feared: was this a prelude to an atomic hostage-taking? A co-ordinated act of sabotage? "Terrorism" (organized surprise violence against civilians as a political lever) was a great bogey in 2006, but evidence later suggested Dark Friday came about through simple consumerist greed, less-than-vigilant overseeing of power sources, and a chilling instance of collusion among computerized management systems. While not *physically* interconnected, a far-flung chain of generators had somehow turned, via the intricate communications webs they fueled into being, a single disruption at one station into the complete shutdown of all of them. Already stretched beyond their capacities, the engines of the network-cities broke down under the very babble they were engineered to amplify. Information had been twisted into a genuine vicious circle.

In the turbulent hours of Dark Friday the immediate fear was of mob rule, of some calamitous societal unrest that would sweep the unlit, unregulated streets—anarchy, in short. Subsequent tales of how this did not occur, of how "tranquility filled the vortex" (as implied in Kaldek's *The Freeing of the Drones*), were quite exaggerated: close to 7,000 fatalities were counted, resulting from assaults as much as accidents and heat exhaustion, and theft and vandalism were widespread. But it was not until power was restored after six hours (suburban areas waited longer) that the deeper consequences of September 15 were realized. The losses in life and property, it transpired, were compounded by abstract losses of valuable information. Enormous transactions of wealth, routinely passed by wire or wireless signals, had been erased when the lights went off; unknowable stocks of research and expression and facts were wiped out in a second. Much of this was certainly retrievable, but a significant portion had been destroyed before it could be fully logged into memory banks. Commercial exchanges, scientific analyses, and artistic, journalistic, and political statements were cut off midway and could neither be properly concluded nor preserved. A single day of turmoil had left the economies of the American Bloc and the European Community shaken and vulnerable to their Asian competitors. Dark Friday, then, became known as a "virtual disaster" (an allusion to the computerized simulations of authentic experience that were fashionable in those years), where the damage and deaths were hardly more severe than the financial and organizational casualties suffered at an artificial level. Two years earlier the world had seen that its masses of treasured Information could not save Volgograd nor even mourn it with any dignity; after September 15, 2006, it appeared that Information could not even save itself.

For over two decades the Volgograd explosion and Dark Friday would remain as cautionary fables to the general public. One had revealed the ultimate impotence of Information in the face of actual tragedy, while the other had illuminated Information's own precariousness and the folly of unhesitating devotion to it. Some institutions moved to scale down their use of technological "improvements" over older, more trustworthy methods and devices, a few abandoned all but the simplest functions of their computers, and many adopted what were believed to be more efficient means of controlling their data resources. In 2018, for example, the Canadian government introduced its decentralization policy, following the lead of private firms which had streamlined their internal communications routes to ad hoc rather than fixed bases. Prime Minister Ingrid Andersen originated the term "organic nationalism" in proposing the idea; its purpose was both to eliminate the risk of another Dark Friday and to "wean the state from its data gluttony," in her words. Andersen and other reformers were the avant-garde of a radical change in the notions of order and democracy—today we are living out their visions.

Culturally, the first impacts of the nuclear and virtual disasters are difficult to perceive, particularly from our distant vantage. On the surface, the pre-eminence of electronic media was still unchallenged, and the communications industry in all its manifestations—from the manufacture of computer apparatus to the retail of Tri-Sense entertainment programs, from the visual music of Nightingale Jones to the popular Random Access Network—was still immensely profitable. At the same time there existed in the private rooms and public parks of the silicon states—within the hearts and minds of those same individuals who were the source of all the info-fortune—what Gedi called "a secret hysteria," a largely unspoken and unacted-upon concern over the transience and cacophony of their world. This concern was by no means a new one; objections to the Information Age's disorienting, impersonal whirl had been raised as far back as the early twentieth century. In the post-Volgograd, post-Dark Friday period, however, people were more aware than ever of the paradox they faced: to condemn Information, they had to contribute to it. Only an inspired few were able to resolve the dilemma—the Opus Rex group (2012–2020), Carmen Jaeger (1998–2098), and the great Yamashiro. For the rest, true liberation was far in the future, and as yet unthinkable.

Little of this mood (such as it was) was obvious to the men and women of the twenty-first century's first half. They were preoccupied with the legacy of their ancestors. The criminal mishandling of the biosphere, the entrenchment of socioeconomic inequities, sputtering regional warfare, narrow-minded land use initiatives (or no initiatives at all), and lax contraceptive standards that were only alarming fifty years previously had become fully cataclysmic. In the 2020s large tracts of Asia, Europe, and the Americas were flooded for weeks at a time: rising ocean levels forced coastal cities in Australia and Oceania to be indefinitely evacuated; and Mexico City, Cairo, Bombay, and other centres were declared "urban wastelands," officially unfit for human residence. 2031 was the year of the Saigon plague, a powerful and mysterious strain of the AIDS disease that ravaged southeast Asia and gained footholds in India and the Latin American Union—in ten months the death toll swelled to almost 1.9 million—before a vaccine was finally developed. In considering bygone generations' neglect and shortsightedness, and the epic misfortunes that were their inheritance, the people of this blighted era would recall the Greek proverb, "The gods visit the sins of the fathers upon the children." Others thought less of blame or guilt and mused instead on the ironic Chinese curse, "May you live in interesting times."

But whatever the philosophical implications of these problems, one thing was becoming more and more evident: Information would not solve them. In a limited sense, unquestionably, the worldwide networks could rapidly disseminate useful material to the men and women—engineers, or medical scientists, say—who were directly combatting this or that case of pollution or disease or malnutrition; overall, though, the bulk of the data carried by any medium held little value against the onslaughts of wounded nature or age-old propensities for mistrust and antagonism. "In Manila, they are dying in the streets," United Nations Secretary-General Lauzon pointed out in 2032. "They do not need Comlink." She may have said the same of those washed out of their homes in St. Louis or Brisbane, of chemical-deformed children born in Tianjin or Novokuznetsk, or of militia gang victims in Los Angeles, Cape Town, or Karachi. Information had become, as Carmen Jaeger depicted in *The First Day of Spring* (2029), "a staple luxury," a currency honoured by all but of worth to few, aged and grown past its prime.

In the United States of America, the disparity between the amount of information being processed when measured against its tangible good had entered the realm of absurdity. Until the 2030s the country's most pressing problems were still identified as variations on the have versus have-not theme, spawning numerous hand-wringings on the "gap" between riches and poverty, which by the turn of the century had been modernized to hand-wringings on the "gap" between "techno-peasants" and "data barons" or "hackerlords." The greatest controversy continued to be focussed on the distribution of wealth, whether financial or intellectual; no one (or nearly no one) had suggested that there may have been too much wealth to begin with.

Thus what lighted the initial fires of the Second American Civil War was, at least in part, a smouldering resentment on the part of millions who felt ignored and disenfranchised by the network nation they lived in. It was not so much that they wanted more information for themselves, or a bigger share of the prosperity it generated—they simply could no longer tolerate the blatant division of inescapable reality and tantalizing image, of painful experience and utopian ideal, of dreary truths and glittering lies. The Atlanta Uprisings of 2036 were of course borne of long-simmering "racial" tensions that had split the land along ethnocentric lines (European, African, Asian, Latino), but it was the abject failure of the world's most Information-opulent society to seriously address the real-life misery within its borders that may have been their true parent. As more violent unrest spread to city after city throughout the republic—eventually to coalesce after the killing of Luther Brown T*R by government agents on January 1, 2037—the less the conflict seemed motivated by long-standing blood feuds as by raw frustration with Information's broken promises.

Some of this only became apparent with hindsight. Two years of death and destruction gutted many communities of the nation, during which most foreign observers saw only a horrendous tribal war: like so many other emergencies of the time, the Second Civil War ostensibly was a predictable climax to the turbulence of centuries past. This was a reasonable enough analysis (the Civil War of 1861–1865 was also fought over issues of race), yet when the fighting finally died more complicated interpretations began to come forth. In *RageRoots* (2041), Arthur Hong asserted that:

> ... the hostilities might not have happened to the degree that they did had the networks not so blithely insisted that they were not happening at all; conversely, there may have been more interest in averting them had their first skirmishes not been reported as titillation comparable to vr erotica or the latest antics of Teesha Gonzales. ... Perhaps the war was

ultimately the act of a nation "getting back to basics," reminding itself in the most vicious way of the fundamental things that Online and the RAN had obscured for years. . . .

In other words, the social, economic, political, and environmental causes of the Second Civil War were obvious enough, but the *cultural* ones, the suffocating triviality of electronic amusement and the clash of televised fictions with concrete facts, were just as important; "I want my MTV" is now as notorious a gesture of ignorant callousness as "Let them eat cake" was long ago. Information, in the end, had to share the blame for a strife that fragmented a country and left one million of its people slain.

While the United States was being rent by its domestic carnage, international rivalries on the other side of the globe were approaching a crisis point. China and India, each densely populated, each beset with ecological and biological disasters, and each vying with Japan and each other for economic dominance of continental Asia, had raised their respective military forces to hair-trigger levels of alertness. Both adversaries had stated their intentions to use nuclear weaponry if provoked, and other governments either could not or would not interfere. By 2039 "Helter Skelter" (the colloquial name for the Second Civil War) had burned out the heartland of North America, and the European Community, the Federal Russian Republic, Australia, and the Latin American Union had assumed isolationist stances: Asia's two strongest war machines were left alone against each other.

Neither the Chinese nor the Indians were as swamped with Information as Americans and Europeans were, but their networks were advanced enough and monopolized enough to stir up jingoist, chauvinist fervour among hundreds of millions—British Prime Minister Vankata remarked that each state was "fostering First Millennium hatreds through Second Millennium means." Indeed, the media-induced belligerence that infested both populations was reminiscent of the nationalist manias of the previous century, manias which had inevitably been preludes to war.

The escalations which culminated in the nuclear attacks on Shanghai and New Delhi, therefore, were the fateful product of geopolitical friction, reckless sabre-rattling, and Informational incitement. Chinese Premier Zhao's decision to launch an atomic strike against the Indian capital on May 16, 2039 was probably engendered by ill-founded skepticism of his enemy's retaliatory capability; similarly, Indian Prime Minister Singh's position was dictated by bullying from her own countrymen as well as from the Chinese themselves. Miraculously, no further warheads were exploded after China's first punch and India's response. The staggering casualties of the blasts—over two million human beings killed in thirty minutes, more than the death tolls of the Volgograd bombing and the Second American Civil War combined—had stopped each nation's military command systems cold. Less than an hour in duration, the Sino-Indian exchange was the worst injury inflicted by the Asian people on themselves since the Second World War, yet the relative mildness of the wound was frighteningly ironic. Luis Ison (2002–2043) eventually compared it to "a man falling from a high precipice only to land in water instead of against stones, scraping his knees rather than breaking his back." To be able to speak of *only* two million people annihilated, as opposed to the billions who were in fact at risk, underscored how much the Exchange had held doom in check.

Worldwide, the reaction was one of mute horror, much as had followed Volgograd's destruction a generation before. But this quiet was also a sign of other nations' exhaustion from their own problems; cross-border pathways of Information were not as well-travelled as they had once been. Network grids still operated, and news and entertainment and data were still sent quickly from continent to continent, but violence, disease, and all manner of upheaval had severely diminished Information's accessibility. A colossal story it may have been, the obliteration of Shanghai and New Delhi nevertheless was described awkwardly, peripherally, in Vancouver and Johannesburg and Sao Paulo and Frankfurt. Recalling Volgograd, journalists and their audiences together sensed the Exchange was beyond the scope of everyday telecommunications—and now there was added the competition from *local* calamities that seemed altogether more urgent than a pair of distant firestorms. Insofar as "Information" meant intelligence sent artificially from faraway places, it was commanding less and less attention. The sorrow of the Sino-Indian Nuclear Exchange of 2039 was not just in the number of lives that were lost, but in the rest of the planet's numbed, vacant comprehension of it.

It was some time after November-December 2043 that the events of those months were summed up as the "Pacific Catastrophe."

History does not present itself ready-made, as serious historians have always sought to remind us, for it is usually only in retrospect that the countless actions on the world stage shape themselves into a salient pattern. That said, however, it did not require much perspective to recognize that the havoc wrought upon the earth between Tuesday, November 10 and Sunday, December 6, 2043, was indeed a single, unspeakable historical milestone. The Pacific Catastrophe was the last, and worst, disaster to befall mankind in the scarred twenty-first century; it also marked the end of the primary stage in the decline of the Age of Information.

In 2048 the newly organized World Parliament enlisted its statisticians to tally the number of casualties left by the Catastrophe. Their figures of nineteen million dead and six million injured were soon denounced as far too conservative—unscientific estimates ran up to twenty-one million injured people (including those bereft of adequate housing, nutrition, and hygiene) and a tenth of a *billion* people killed. Economic losses were in every sense beyond calculation. The twentieth century's Second World War and Cold War, and the Second American Civil War of 2036–2038, had likely incurred only a fraction of the Pacific Catastrophe's financial damage. Eventually the magnitude of the debacle was deemed by Congressional Officer Ernestina Storig to be "without measure and blasphemed by number-crunching."

Briefly, the Pacific Catastrophe was the series of seismic shocks which struck at several points along the western coasts of North and South America, at the Japanese home islands, in northeast Asia, and at Oceania, during a three-week period in the fall of 2043. These earthquakes—as well as attendant volcanic

activity—set off widespread devastation from collapsing structures, fires, chemical and nuclear leakage, and a general break-
down of social order, and these in their turn were aggravated by
conditions of overpopulation and internal decay that were already
extant.

Like a cosmic game of chance, the huge tremors and eruptions seemed to decimate at random. While the geologic boundaries of the earth's crust and the "earthquake zones" that were
strung across the globe had been familiar for over a century, no
reliable means of predicting quakes had been devised. There
could thus have been no expectation of the sudden occurrence of
so many massive disturbances in so short a time (a blink of an eye,
geologically): educated guesswork had only deduced the "Ring of
Fire" that belted the Pacific Ocean, noted tectonic fault lines, and
identified the locations of possible future epicentres. Occasional
instances of earthquakes and volcanic eruptions, though they had
killed many thousands of people, had done so over many decades,
so it was assumed they would continue to do so at the same
"manageable," irregular pace. Instead, what happened in 2043
was simply a case of far too much, far too quickly.

Beginning—deceptively—in the modestly populated Aleu-
tian Islands, the gargantuan seismic spasms went back and forth
around the ocean. Earthquakes visited Guatemala next; then Bu-
lusan erupted in the northern Philippine island of Luzon; the
terrible Californian and Peruvian quakes followed, two days
apart; Villarrica spewed fire and ash over southern Chile; the
Chinese metropolis of Tangshan was rocked; the Kamchatkan
Peninsula's Bezymianny exploded; and finally the cities of the

main Japanese island of Honshu toppled in an earthquake of
stunning ferocity. The scale of these was apocalyptic. To those
touched by them, they appeared to be nothing less than the end
of the world, and observers elsewhere could barely organize a
portion of the relief measures that were needed. As well, the
Catastrophe did not end with natural blows—later World Parliament studies concluded that as many as two-thirds of the dead
were victims of "man-made" ruin. Industrial, military, and corporate installations, power stations, transportation hubs, medical
facilities, and public works infrastructures were shattered along
with ordinary dwellings, magnifying the crises enormously. In the
places struck hardest, civilization itself had figuratively and virtually fallen to pieces.

The aftermath of the Pacific Catastrophe—the "smoke,
rubble, death" of Li's song cycle—saw most of the world's people
enrolled, in some fashion or other, to provide aid for the helpless
regions bordered around the vast ocean. Emergency food, shelter,
and makeshift hospitals were delivered, and survivors of radioac-
tive and toxic spills—where there were survivors at all—were
rescued. National armed forces had to replace police departments
in areas plagued with crime epidemics; health and sanitation
services, too, were in desperate demand.

Prioritization was imperative. The tasks set before humanity were formidable, and they had to be undertaken in order of
greatest necessity. First came the disposal of the dead, either
through burial, or, more commonly, incineration; then there was
the restoration of basic medical ministration and law and order;
longer-range planners set about—eventually—rebuilding com-

munities and reclaiming lost or poisoned land. Daunting as these projects were (and some seemed plainly hopeless), there was one problem they were not complicated by: the disablement of the information networks. Not only was the repair of global communications systems not considered of any urgency, many involved in the relief work—that is, many millions of men, women, and children—believed that the lack of intact systems was a help rather than a hindrance to their efforts. The Pacific Catastrophe, and the catastrophes that preceded it, had to be fully faced and fully remedied. A suspicion had developed that Information was not a cure but part of the original disease.

This is not the story of the heroic healing programs that reshaped the world for over a hundred years from the middle of the twenty-first century, of names like Kamali, Dunn, Dadmanesh, Asaoka, or Mohan, of the waves of emigration and resettlement that redistributed the world's population to an extent unseen since two centuries before; those sagas have deservedly been told many times. What is relevant to us is not mankind's determined advance against adversity, but its equally resolute retreat from excess. Information was now to sink from being a symbol of unmet potential to being an inducement of unmatched remorse.

After great pain, a formal feeling comes—
The Nerves sit ceremonious, like Tombs—
The stiff Heart questions was it He, that bore,
And Yesterday, or Centuries before?

The Feet, mechanical, go round—
Of ground, or Air, or Ought—
A Wooden way
Regardless grown,
A Quartz contentment, like a stone—

This is the Hour of Lead—
Remembered, if outlived,
As Freezing persons, recollect the Snow—
First—Chill—then Stupor—then the letting go—
                    —Emily Dickinson, untitled, 1862

CHAPTER TWO

The Great Shame

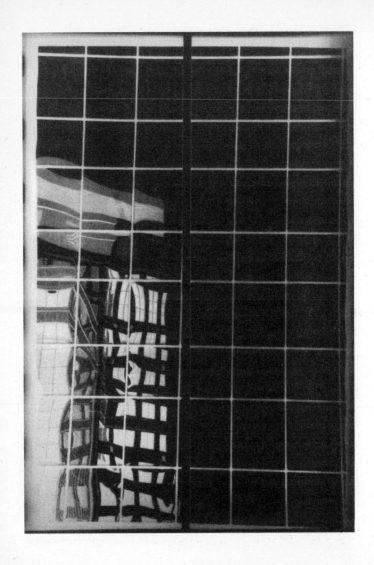

t was the African philosopher Gedi (circa 2030–2110) who both described and epitomized the second phase of the Information Age's slow deterioration. He was born, lived, and died knowing mostly material scarcity, caring little for possessions or achievement, and never directly recorded his thoughts in any medium. There are only two authenticated photographs of him. His teachings were originally spoken to his immediate family and neighbours, who repeated them verbatim to a widening range of outsiders. Gradually, transcriptions of his statements were made and collected for mass dissemination, but from several sources and revealing several (not always consistent) themes. No money went to Gedi from the sale of these documents, and in fact scant profit was made by anyone involved in their distribution. For all the familiarity of his work, his personal renown was small. As such, he is an ideal emblem of the era in which the world, like a maturing child, began to outgrow its Informational toys: as Gedi put it, "This is the time of the great shame."

The shame, to be sure, did not set in overnight. Information continued to be created, processed, transmitted, and stored in impressive volumes. There were still silicon states, and information technology was still produced and consumed; none of it could be deinvented or magically rendered inoperable. But there were also many places where it *was* inoperable—Tokyo, Los Angeles, New Delhi, Shanghai, Miami, Manila, San Francisco, Saigon, Santiago, Chicago, Lima, and all the parts of the planet where the fundamental composition of society had come undone. In these locales the need for Information, or the lack of need, was not even an issue. The very things that made it possible—electricity, hardware, software, and most importantly, human life—had been wiped out.

And aside from *physical* incapacitation, Information (or at any rate the most extravagant uses of it) had taken on an ethical stigma as well. As early as the Volgograd and Dark Friday episodes, the mass media's moral failings had been apparent, and each successive bout of troubles had accelerated its obsolescence. No longer was it necessary to risk hypocrisy in attacking Information by manipulating Information itself, for now, with so many systems wrecked or fallen into disuse, it was easier and more effective simply to ignore it. Here Gedi's influence was most distinct, as well as that of the anonymous thousands whose blunt graffito, deeds not words, was a ubiquitous slogan scrawled on countless surfaces throughout the world.

Thus, between a new social temperament and the tough new actualities of day-to-day life, the defining trends of the period took shape. For example, the international economic reconfiguration (then referred to as a "depression") which followed the Second Civil War and gained momentum after the Pacific

Catastrophe ensured less expenditure on advertisements and other auxiliaries of production which made up "corporate culture." Couple this with the near-total disintegration of major communications centres in California, Japan, and India—headquarters for the production and management of nearly half of all the world's cultural output, in terms of market size and value—and the result was a decline both in the amount of information available and the number of people who were willing to pay to receive it.

Likewise, the impairment of the Information industry and the guilt felt by those who had survived years of tragedy combined to alter the tone of the material that did reach a general audience. Again, this was an ongoing movement, insofar as people had long seen a rude discrepancy between Information's garish impermanence and the primal validity of real life: this was one of the roots of Helter Skelter. But by 2050 there was so much to be done with such solemnity of purpose that there was little public appetite whatsoever for the vulgar diversions that had made up the bulk of recorded knowledge since the nineteenth century. The emphasis shifted by degrees to practical, straightforward subject matter that was devoid of hyperbole or pandering—the widely read journal *Alpha*, full of ecological tips, encouragements to civic participation, and the charming wisdom of "Junebug," was representative of this.

To their credit, the hundreds of millions of citizens who were curbing their Informational intakes did not have to resort to active denial to do so. The traditions of civil liberty and democratic government that had sprung from the Renaissance were still observed in the new millennium by a majority of political bodies, including the World Parliament. "Freedom of the press," or "free speech" (*speech* and *the press* being generic appellations for any communication form), continued to be respected and enforced; there was no censorship. The abandonment by entire populations of a given network (or publication, or performer, or program, or genre of art, or spectacle, or style of dress), then, was literally an abandonment. Men and women everywhere still held the right to *choose* crass sensationalism over pure edification, an option they had exercised more often than not in the past—but in the mid-twenty-first century, men and women began to choose differently. As Julius La Cerra (2014–2086) wrote in *Alpha*:

> We have come to realize that free speech doesn't mean only that the *state* cannot restrict what we have to say, but also that *nothing* can: not avarice, nor fear, nor vanity, nor ignorance, nor lust, nor any of the mental fetters that once bound expression as firmly as legal ones. *Truly* free speech must be the voice of the entire individual rather than his superficial impulses.

Well apart from aesthetic reform, the Great Shame also saw a wholesale discarding of much logistic and technical information. Once more, something that had been tried in partial steps for decades became more fully implemented; once more, the impetus was both necessity *and* virtue, an ultimate awakening to what *could* be done and what *should* be done. So any research, statistic, datum or measurement that gave no meaningful service was, over time, scrapped. Ingrid Andersen's work of the 2020s was coming to fruition. Government censuses, consumer studies, redundant or ill-defined scientific inquiries, most financial tabulations, and infinite bureaucratic regulations were decided to be a waste of resources, or all too obviously had no more function (how to poll shoppers or calculate profits or count fauna in the ruins of Honshu or Shanghai?). Industrial design, medical investigation, environmental reporting, and record-keeping of any consequence, on the other hand, would not have to compete with mere "noise" to use or become information. In academia, too, instructors and their pupils alike recognized the need to teach and learn utilitarian skills rather than more speculative disciplines—though rarely were explicit changes legislated, public and private educators and societies at large arrived at a mutual objective to distinguish vital information from frivolous. This did not mean, as some had worried, that the humanities would be forsaken for the hard sciences, but that all fields of learning were understood to have less to draw on materially, intellectually, and economically than before, and should restrain themselves accordingly. Now schools, no less than political, mercantile, or military enterprises, no less than all social organizations, withdrew from their Information habits. It was done voluntarily, but it was, in the end, mandatory.

From 2060 to the first years of the twenty-second century the communications industry was trimmed, through accident and design, to a fraction of the size it had been a hundred years before. It still *was* an industry, certainly, just as it in some senses remains one to this day, and it is not always easy to appreciate how bloated it was at its peak. Using technology to relay knowledge of all types, to trade wealth, services, and commodities, and to offer entertainment, continued to be (and still is) a customary practice, but the Great Shame curtailed that practice immensely. A stern delineation was made between "hard info" and "soft," between intelligence that contributed in one way or another to the good of everyone and that which did not, between the personal, considered statements of creative individuals and the largely fabricated "culture" dispensed and controlled by monolithic businesses, and above all between true experience and cheap forgeries of it, or convoluted responses to those forgeries. At last, Information was sorting itself out instead of multiplying unchecked.

A landmark in this process of reevaluation was Sari Turek's mammoth history *Five Hundred Channels, Fifteen Minutes* (2073). The twelve-hour electronic opus took a bitterly critical—albeit carefully detailed—view of Information at its most decadent, during the twentieth century. While noting the greatest artistic achievements of the time—the moving images of Chaplin and Disney, and the music of the Beatles, to name three—Turek showed how rare such brilliance was among endless quantities of trite "product"; she pointed out the futile obsession with celebrity and novelty that then marked society, and how little-perceived was the fact of most Information's being essentially a retail item sold by a few monopolies at inflated prices to a gullible public. Easily the better part of it all, Turek concluded, was quite worthless to civilization's well-being. "That it was allowed to run so rampant," her narrator intoned, "is an indictment of the human race."

Five Hundred Channels, Fifteen Minutes contained many

examples of Information's most outrageous tangents, its most inconsequential VR programs, television plays, journalism, computer games, magazines, books, motion pictures, scholarly papers, and so on—they were only slightly more obtainable for Sari Turek in the 2070s than they are to us now, consigned as they are to thousands of deserted warehouses, vaults, and filing centres around the world. Some of these were definitely lost in the Pacific Catastrophe and other cataclysms, but most have survived. No one owns them, except as physical objects (that is, paper, discs, recording tape, photographic film, and the like); they are unclaimed and unwanted relics of a disgraced past.

If what Ingrid Andersen had called "data gluttony" was a hunger slowly being reined in, the more general economic voracity of the world had been put on a spartan diet indeed. Information, after all, was industrial output not unlike harvested raw materials or manufactured goods, and its diminution was but one aspect of the overall changes taking place in world finance. Dealt mortal blows from fifty years of virtual, natural, and military armageddons, the giants of capital and commerce held no more authority over the global economy. The more that was owned, either by human tycoons or networked conglomerates, the more they had lost; such, ultimately, was the monetary result of five troubled decades. Complete accounts of the recovery and conversion, as remarked previously, have filled many volumes. Suffice it to say here that, from 2050 onward, the first groping advances towards our current Worldwealth were made—learning from the often abominable mistakes of both capitalism and socialism, public officials, private entrepreneurs, and popular advocates struggled to assemble the principles of ownership, fiscal policy, sustenance laws, and other economic bases of today's society. Carlos Majara (2021–2104) described them as a prescription for "collective competition," while Le Liu's *Theory of Cooperative Anarchy* (2085) codified them further.

These movements, embryonic and trial-and-error though they were, put more pressure on the slowly crumbling Information Age. As the most stagnant industrial rivalries and least-needed consumer goods became extinct, their attendant promotional fanfares died also. To repeat, corporate culture had been withering since the Second American Civil War, but towards the end of the twenty-first century its extended offshoots were decaying as well. So deeply had commercial interests permeated the daily affairs of civilization, their recession affected nearly everyone. Beyond the straightforward facts that, compared to the preceding century, there was less information being merely merchandised and more of it held some moral or intellectual value, the makeup of society itself was being reshaped. It was left to a hitherto obscure European writer to characterize the revolution she and her fellow citizens were in the midst of.

Keranka Djondovic's *The Eclipse of Pluralism* (2079) is in its own fashion as important a philosophical creation as those of Gedi: whether or not she observed a genuine social trend or (as her detractors claimed) only prompted it into being, there is little doubt that her brief study, available in numerous media, has become one of the conclusive pronouncements of the Great Shame. Its central thesis was that local and global devastations had stunned mankind into a heightened level of classlessness, and that artificial, cosmetic distinctions among people had lost most of their admission. The worth of "pluralistic" or "heterogeneous" communities, she claimed, had been so demeaned that contemporary folk were now reversing the standards of their forebears and upholding unity and mutuality—no longer diversity and insularity—as social ideals; demographic expanses which had once been regarded as invigorating at best and tolerable at worst were denounced by Djondovic as outright evils. She called them "the castes of the damned."

The Eclipse of Pluralism was not saying that people had become indistinguishable from one another. Fundamental differences of gender, genetics, personal qualities, and personal ideologies were recognized and held to be, the author supposed, "probably timeless"—a prediction borne out to anyone noting the Arctic Debates of 2463–65! But Djondovic depicted a world where petty idiosyncrasies of temperament and biology had become insignificant, especially since many of them had been dictated or encouraged by a consumptive market economy that was now severely eroded. Some of the poorer Asian, African, and Latin American nations had always known a type of "necessary uniformity"; it was in the richer lands that women and men, by 2079, had adopted the "egalitarian option." If egalitarianism truly *was* an option is questionable, since there was then far less means to pursue assorted "lifestyles." More convincing was Djondovic's illustration of the bizarre popular extremes pluralism had once inspired: competing sects had defined themselves according to age, colour, sexuality, income, ethnic or regional affiliation, and even taste in clothing, entertainment, and intoxicants. It was suggested that:

> ... not only had these senseless demarcations fos-
> tered the hostilities that brought about Helter Skelter
> and other clashes, but they had also sapped the demo-
> cratic spirit and debased it into fodder for opportun-
> ists, hucksters, and cynics of every stripe. This was a
> profound betrayal of the very principles of liberty and
> equality that allowed polycult societies to begin with.

Despite its scathing assessment of societal corruptions, *The Eclipse of Pluralism* was an optimistic work, for it pointed to a renewed simplicity and commonality of outlook throughout the world. No longer driven by governments or businesses and industries—least of all the Information industry—to segregate themselves along fabricated boundaries, people were coalescing in a striking global harmony. It was the first indication of an even more impressive union that was to come.

Keranka Djondovic, like Sari Turek and Gedi and other thinkers, was describing a process that was imperceptible from one day to the next. She and her peers had identified general drifts of history, not specific historical events. But the Great Shame ultimately was encapsulated by a single achievement, the impor-tance of which was plain to all who contributed to it: the election of Ramona Herrington to the American presidency on November 4, 2104.

While the office itself had declined in power next to that of the World Parliamentary representative, evolved as it was to a position of national administration more than supranational leadership, it was still keenly contested. Herrington's victory over her rivals Paolo Benwell and Jennifer Shih was, on its own, only of moderate impact. Her far greater symbolic triumph was to be voted in without using electronic media—information technology—as a campaign tool. Other political candidates before and during her race had relied more on public appearances than recorded presentations, but Herrington's electoral support had been garnered almost solely through face-to-face encounters with citizens across the country, eschewing more sophisticated vote-getting tactics.

The election was certainly *documented* by the few networks that continued to operate, as professional journalists and amateur observers continued to detail its facts and note the opinions which surrounded it, but their influence had been diminished. A majority of Americans had little or no access to anything but the most basic news sources (mostly inexpensive publications or short-range broadcasting stations), and those who had more were less inclined to depend on them as primary or objective purveyors of facts. Ramona Herrington's winning strategy, then, was to distance herself from discredited communications systems: spreading political messages through loosely organized rallies, impromptu speechmaking, and word of mouth worked much better for her than means that were themselves already distrusted. It was a physically draining way to run for office, but it proved far more appealing to voters.

Restrained, dignified, and purposeful, the 2104 elections

became a landmark of a nation's shuffling off its Informational coils, and its implications were seen around the world. Herrington's actual policies—aimed at completing the restoration work begun following the Second Civil War and upset again by the Pacific Catastrophe—were laudable enough, but more public acclaim went to her as a candidate and to her newly emancipated countrymen. For more than a century ballots in many states had been heavily orchestrated affairs in which a relatively slight number of eligible voters had taken part, and whose outcomes were more or less predetermined by biased news reporting, direct or indirect bribery, and massively funded promotional campaigns that "sold" office-seekers to a benighted electorate; at the dawn of the twenty-second century the environment in which such factors flourished was no more, and so the American presidential vote was probably the freest and most participatory in the republic's history. Even Herrington's competitor Jennifer Shih conceded that it stood for "the rise of the democratic phoenix." It was a vindication of all the progressive and reflective beliefs that had arisen in the aftermath of the disaster years. The shame had gone deep, but humanity was showing that it had learned a valuable lesson from it.

There was neither an official opening or close of the Great Shame—it was (and still is) a general characterization for a lengthy cultural change that very slowly came over the earth. Its relevance here is in its signifying a sweeping *volte-face* in human consciousness, the swing away from living by the overtly material and rational bounties of technology and reason towards things less concrete, less *constructed*. The Information Age itself was a logical end to the route civilization had wandered since Gutenburg and Newton and Copernicus and Columbus had set out on their voyages of cerebral and physical discovery; now civilization had turned around and was back again at the place where the paths had first diverged, and was about to venture down the other way. The only thing left to do was take a final glance backward. That final glance became the first step.

Any sufficiently advanced technology is indistinguishable from magic.

—Arthur C. Clarke, *The Lost Worlds of 2001*, 1972

CHAPTER THREE

Science's Last Stand

have achieved some success with the project," Grant McIvor entered into his computer on April 12, 2138, "but I will need more than a usual number of independent verifications." The slight, retiring European physicist was an irrepressible tinkerer and lover of gadgets, but he was also possessed of a gruff skepticism and a firm sense of the practical—the heritage of his dour Scottish ancestors?—and he knew he would have to demonstrate his new invention in front of a substantial audience before it would ever be accepted by the scientific community, or the ordinary person. He had, after all, developed a means by which solid objects could be sent from one point to another without a secondary carrying agent—"in and out of thin air," he wrote, "the sleight-of-hand of ancient magicians and tricksters become hard reality."

McIvor made the first public display of his experiment at the University of Edinburgh on April 27. He referred to it dryly as his "Corporeal Transmission Method," though it was more accurate to call it a device; our own term of *teleportation* did not come into use for some time. Once his fellow researchers confirmed that he had indeed sent physical things—a brick, a board, a stone, and his own tie—from the central engineering laboratory to a lecture hall in another building, and returned them intact the same way, McIvor became an international sensation. At first much of the acclaim he received centred on his being an "eccentric genius," a stubborn dreamer toiling in solitude, without governmental or corporate sponsorship, not unlike the inventors Watt, Bell, or Nakazawa. Only when the first primitive teleportation units started to operate at more and more places around the world did the enormity of McIvor's achievement begin to overshadow the personal standing of its creator.

We at the prelude to the twenty-sixth century, for whom "corporeal transmission" has been an everyday occurrence for generations, easily forget how it appeared to the men and women of 2138. Though some of the principles Grant McIvor made use of were vaguely known as theoretical possibilities for a few decades before his work took shape, historically they were regarded as amusing daydreams rather than real avenues for technological development. Artists of speculative fiction had often imagined teleportation-like instruments, to the indulgent delight of their followers, but when people first witnessed genuine teleportation in action, delight was replaced by sheer amazement, and even, among a few holdouts, determined suspicion of fraud. Eventually, once teleportation had proved its utilitarian worth, humanity recognized it as the ultimate tool ever to have been at its disposal.

The invention's novelty soon wore off: laymen as well as expert professionals clearly understood that it was not a toy nor a fad but a supremely useful form of transportation. Because its basic components were relatively inexpensive, and because McIvor gladly sold his design to all who sought it, teleportation rapidly took over the shipping and delivery industries. By 2145 any simple inanimate object—an electronic filament, a silicon particle, a concrete block, a sheet of paper, a steel girder—could be sent to the other side of the planet in a few minutes, and the great teleportation staging-bases at Tucson, Casablanca, and Singapore were being constructed. Congressional Officer Kirby Mohan authorized the installation of the World Transmission Lanes in 2149 and devised the Standard Sending Rates—while seldom were they strictly adhered to, the wtls and ssrs provided "choice passage" to material and their agents directly involved in the ecological and civil restoration programs still underway. Clumsy and limited from a modern perspective—early element waves could not accommodate composite or biological material—teleportation had nevertheless forever altered the mechanics of social and economic interaction.

But there was another change brought about by the invention. Information, its influence and scope dwindling as it was, lost even more import after McIvor. Its old exponents (or more precisely, its vested-interest propagandists) had always extolled its elevation over messy physical experience, its ability to somehow remove its users from cluttered reality by the use of streamlined symbols for, or representations of, that reality. This was correct inasmuch as it was meaningful to describe two hundred and fifty-six separate units as "256," say, or to use a pocket-sized map as an accurate model of a great geographical range: this was how language and images had become fixtures of human understanding. But teleportation went a step further than Information ever had. Instead of the long-distance conveyance of what were essentially *ideas* (standardized arrangements of written characters, pictures, sounds, or electronic impulses) being the pinnacle of technological power, it was now *things themselves* that could be conveyed. Instead of being a conceptualized, portable facsimile of real life, Information was further along the way to being seen as merely a poor substitute for it.

Even if, in the middle of the twenty-second century, it was still far more convenient for men and women to communicate via Information rather than teleportation, the possibilities raised by the new instruments cast an intimidating shadow over the consciousness of society. In 2160 a citizen of Oslo, Europe could in principle have a face-to-face dialogue with a friend in Nairobi, Africa, could share soulful glances, soothing voices, pages of textual data, and even (provided the right equipment was available) sexual contact—but they would all be apprehended as only *approximations* of personal exchange, mere *simulations* of a true encounter. Even supposing an Oslo-Nairobi Informational intercourse (and in 2160 such networked, individual-to-individual conversations had long become infrequent), how much more impressive would be Mr. Oslo's ability to, almost instantly, send Ms. Nairobi a handful of pebbles from outside his door, or a silver bracelet, or a length of string she needed, or a drinking mug to replace the one that had just slipped from her hand? The psychological effects of such potential were daunting. Whatever purposes teleportation actually served, the very fact of its existence necessitated a rethinking of what was meant by intellect and invention and technology, of all that they could offer and all that they could not.

Toward the end of the twenty-second century teleportation, already playing a dominant role in civil reconstruction efforts, could also lay claim to the world's popular imagination. The consensus was that it was a feat of almost mythical grandeur, well beyond earlier developments like vaccines or powered flight or nuclear energy. "Ought we to call this the epoch of the ion channel? The century of McIvor? Are the masters of transmission the masters of us all?" Nash Sodhi asked her ally Zephyr in 2191. The governor's questions were rhetorical, but they reflected the mood of dislocation that hung over the earth's eleven billion inhabitants. She may well have also asked the deepest question whose answer no one could guess at: Where do we go from here?

There is more, historically, to the spread of teleportation than its effects on the Information Age, but those effects were certainly among its most serious. If teleportation was decisively "better" than Information—more advanced as a theory and more fundamental in its practice—it was still the product of a similarly materialist, linearist civilization. Once teleportation became routine, even anticlimactic, Information was all the more pedestrian. Televisions and computers and their accessories continued to serve society in numerous ways, but they were not the forefront of a new culture anymore; they were the rear guard of an old one. In 2146 Kirby Mohan had perhaps seen most clearly what teleportation was, or would be, when he told the world, "This may not be science's final triumph, but rather science's last stand."

Mohan's misgivings were echoed by Grant McIvor himself.

Before his death in 2199 at the age of 107 he made a number of public comments that alluded to the finite, fettered nature of teleportation. He did not regret his efforts, he said, and he was proud of the indisputable success and influence his work had had worldwide. But the scientist also pointed out that the development of elemental carrying was part of a continuum that extended back to the developments of navigation, electricity, and atomic physics—"No more than the culmination of a thousand years of labour and ingenuity and persistence, a lineage of brainchildren whose parents were far abler than I." Thus did the man who introduced the marvel of the physical world assess his legacy. McIvor's modesty, we may see, lowered the curtain on one act in the human drama and set the stage for the next.

The Age of Information was nearing its end.

Man is not the centre of the universe as once we thought in our simplicity, but something much more wonderful—the arrow pointing the way to the final unification of the world. . . .

—Pierre Teilhard De Chardin,
The Phenomenon of Man, 1946

CHAPTER FOUR

Omega Horizons

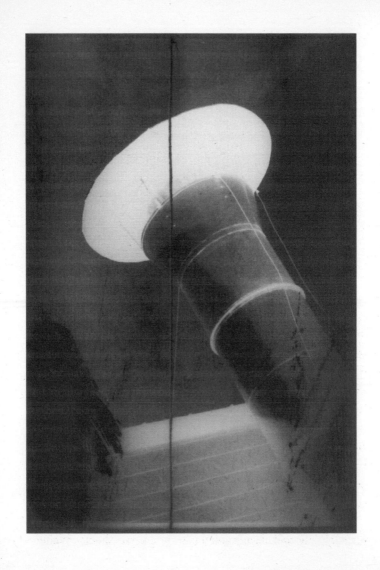

As late as the first decades of the twenty-first century, it was generally supposed that the final destiny of the human species was an eventual merging of man and machine. The evidence at hand suggested so: crude attempts to "alter" the physical makeup of *homo sapiens* to become more compatible with electronic or other devices had already been made, and an alternate possibility was offered by the science of biological engineering, through which the normal processes of the body might be adapted to survive under various "unliveable" conditions. Advocates of such work claimed theirs was only an obvious new level in the advancement of civilization. Women and men had long since learned to live with and benefit from the numberless tools they had devised over the centuries, and they had also been supremely aided by medicine, by ever more sophisticated antitoxins and treatments that allowed them to exist and thrive in often hostile environments. Why, then, the scientists asked, should we not continue further?

If the experiments that resulted from this sort of thinking seem ghastly and deeply inhumane to us, we should remind ourselves that the Information Age was at its height when the new millennium opened, and most of the world's people had concluded an ultimate synthesis of humanity and technology was inevitable. Computer programs were being designed to mimic human characteristics, and individuals were increasingly encouraged to think and live in manners most conducive to the efficient operation of mechanical, electronic, and digital systems. Little wonder, then, that the citizens of the earth were waiting for and working toward a bio-techno renaissance. In hindsight it appears grotesque—at the time it held the hope of a foreordained utopia.

Then, over a span of two centuries, the hope was cruelly dashed. The unutterable visitations of death and disaster, the horrified backing away from Informational omnipotence, and the peculiarly qualified success of teleportation forced an abandonment of technophile ideals, and the most freakish sciences they had fostered were left to stagnate. What would replace them? An intriguing new social direction provided a clue.

In 2208 the World Parliament's Population Assessment observed almost incidentally that spiritual belief and practice continued to be viable aspects of cultural identity among billions; later, independent investigations asserted that the chaos of the twenty-first century and the subsequent global diaspora had produced a curious commingling of ancestral faiths, as mono- and polytheistic and animist religious traditions met and influenced each other in a myriad of instances around the planet. *The Eclipse of Pluralism* was proving truer than its author Djondovic had envisioned. Modest by any contemporary measure, these trends must nonetheless be apprehended as the first stirrings of what we call the Community of Soul.

They were also very different from their ancient origins. Even early into the third millennium, established forms of worship—however free or enlightened they were purported to be—were greatly compromised by their social, political, or economic circumstances, and only a tiny handful of adherents had ever attained any genuinely higher states of consciousness through them. Pared of their antiquated trappings in the twenty-third century, though, without bases in regional, plainly secular situations, their core truths were at last becoming accessible to almost everyone.

Timeworn, customary notions of evil and wrongdoing had not been forgotten, nor had the values of good or virtuous action. But the gradual awakening of spirit that permeated those times did not bring on a return to superstitions or doctrinal rigidities either. Instead hitherto unsuspected or unused sensitivities were introduced into the lives of men, women, and children around the earth. Codes of ethics and morality were not lost but expanded, absorbed by a broader law of awareness and understanding.

Broader indeed. By the mid-2200s a transitory by-product of evolving creed and cognizance was the phenomenon of "documentary redundancy," quaint to current minds but confounding then: it was becoming clear that the official and semiofficial recognitions of popular evolution somehow lagged well behind its actual pace and could not fully articulate its depth. Names and dates and general knowledge appeared on-screen as superfluous details of readily apparent reality. Where we have learned to avoid duplicating or triplicating or mistranslating statements between natural and artificial media, the first generations of the Community were still using Information to tell them what they already knew.

That said, it should not be supposed (as is too often the case nowadays) that Tanis Leung, KI, or Aleila were mere figureheads, or that the Australian or Hemispheric Declarations or the Gaia Charter were formalities, individuals, and events committed to record in every way as afterthoughts, long after the real transitions they are credited with making were complete. In fact it is easy to overlook how important such records were and still are. Latter-day opinion has stereotyped *all* chronicled material pre-dating the Community of Soul as empty and embellished. It is probably instinctive for many of us to sense rather than scrutinize remote eras, to ignore their particulars in favour of their wider aura. But the people and titles that became famous then deserve to be remembered now; their eminence is justified. The old purveyors of Information that hailed them may no longer hold our regard, but their place in the discipline of history—the careful and detached study of the past, as opposed to imprecise and subjective conceptions of it—continues to demand our respect.

How *can* the rise of human comprehension be fully conveyed to readers of the twenty-fifth century? How can the backwardness of pre-Community society be accurately depicted? It is perhaps most important at the outset to acknowledge that the psychic insight which encompasses modern civilization differs only in extent, not in kind, from insight that had *always* been possible for advanced forms of life on earth to experience. It did not come out of nowhere. Over thousands of years it had taken many forms and many designations, and was almost always fleeting and imperfect, but the intangible, isolated inferences that haunted the world for ages are the same ones that joined into the intangible commonwealth where we securely reside today.

As noted previously, the direct antecedent of the Community of Soul, though hardly the only one, was religion. The global spiritual revival that gathered momentum from 2210 onwards was partly derived from the long-held themes of holiness, divinity, transcendence, mysticism and revelation that were found one way or another in every belief structure through history. It was the *idea* of religion, more than its various *ideals*, that was the vital link. As Hagen put it, "The human capacities to think the abstract and feel the sacred became the basic literacy demanded of the new race."

Other primal forces contributed. Dreams and dementia, intuition and emotion, the miracle of birth and the mystery of death, all were lessons in Soul, taught over the eons. The sense of aesthetics, the ability to be moved by beauty in art or nature; the ability to wonder over the surreal or the uncanny, the power of romantic or familial love, the uniqueness of each mind and yet the collective unconscious; the timeless, inexpressible qualities of existence were becoming one. Even the absurdities that provoked laughter or the transient wisdom induced through drugs or alcohol ("In vino veritas") had been primitive manifestations of the Community. Random and alone, any of these were simply the stuff of life for all sentient beings. But imagine them brought together, felt constantly and simultaneously by everyone, and the magnitude of humanity's transfiguration may be grasped.

Self-declared seers from antiquity had sometimes stumbled upon traces of the coming age, only to distort them with the Informational jargon that was their parlance. Often the omens were striking—often they were rendered banal by the crass ulterior motives, usually greed, of those who witnessed and divulged them. If there *was* a prophet of the Community of Soul—a single person who knew and told of its approach—it was the twentieth-century thinker Pierre Teilhard de Chardin (1881–1955). Teilhard was a European Christian, a paleontologist, and a priest of the Jesuit order of the Catholic Church, who theorized that life on Earth was moving in a process toward a universal completion he called "Omega Point." As evinced by his dual callings of science and religion, he believed that matter and spirit were but temporarily divided components of a single, profounder entity, drawing closer together over the millennia. Eventually, Teilhard proposed, they would merge through human consciousness stimulated by Christian love; his reverence of Jesus Christ the Son of God is his particular cultural bias, but it is not incompatible with his essential message. In *My Fundamental Vision* (1948) he wrote:

> If it is true. . . that the human social phenomenon is simply the higher form assumed on earth by the involution of the cosmic stuff upon itself, then we must accept a conclusion for which the road has been prepared by the emergence (already adumbrated in the sciences) of a *Weltanschauung* common to the consciousness of all mankind. (By this we must un-

derstand a vision of the world in which passion plays as large a part as intellect, a vision glowing with the magical nimbus of all that art and poetry have gradually accumulated.) By this I mean that we must recognize the rapidly increasing probability that we are approaching a *critical point of maturity*, at which man, now completely reflecting upon himself not only individually but collectively, will have reached, along the complexity axis (and this with the full force of his spiritual impact), the extreme limit of the world. And it is then, if we wish to attribute a significant direction to our experience and see where it leads, that it seems we are obliged to envisage in that direction, finally to round off the phenomenon, the ultimate emergence of thought on earth into what I have called Omega Point.

In passages such as these Teilhard shows himself to be a remarkably accurate oracle, and his portrayal of what he named the "noosphere"—"the pan-terrestrial organism in which, by compression and arrangement of the thinking particles, a resurgence of evolution (itself now become reflective) is striving to carry the stuff of the universe towards the higher conditions of a planetary super-reflection"—is also an arresting forecast of the Community of Soul. Granting, of course, that nothing like an Omega Point has yet been reached, that no *definitive* wholeness of the world's people has been achieved, we may nevertheless applaud Teilhard's daring inspiration. His imaginings into the future were further and wiser and more sincere than any of his contemporaries'.

From its inception the Community sought a cohesive mandate, a concise constitution that would explain its existence and fortify its place in human activity. This required formal manifestos, publicly validated through all agencies, including Information; organization and organizers were necessary and, again, it is only recently that they have come to be unfairly looked upon with skepticism or dismissal. The citizenry of the era were surprisingly wary of their fresh gifts of perception, and they were compelled to interpret their transcendent alignment with one another in old-style political terms. Documentary redundancy was the persistent handicap then. Many people simply did not trust their senses and could not conceive of a civic system that was not held together by even the barest bureaucracy—at the other extreme, there were those who were eager to cast off not just outmoded fixtures of government (such as the World Parliament) but the very idea of private identity itself. "Surrender to the void" was often urged in the twenty-third century, as was "Overthrow ego." The sources of these somewhat sinister appeals are still unknown. Eventually humanity struck a balance between mass self-negation and conventionally regulated, circumscribed sociality, and the subsequent course of history was charted.

Tanis Leung (2227–2320) and her companion KI (2222–2301) were partners in the Community's entrenchment. In the middle years of the century they issued a number of digital and printed statements testifying to the veracity of spiritual unification, and their home in Resistencia, Latin America, became a hub of Informational and intuitive discourse. As well, Leung and KI were among the architects of the Australian Declaration of 2267, the original endorsement of a general population's psychic sovereignty.

The Australian Declaration served as the model for the Hemispheric Declaration (2272) and the Gaia Charter (2280) which furthered and consolidated the dominion of the Community of Soul (the phrase itself was agreed upon after Telepathic Unity, World Synthesis, and The All were considered). Both Declarations and the Charter were felt to be procedurally vital steps—KI described them as "giving witness before the court of Knowledge"—and their familiar poetry ("Sisters and brothers of the dawn . . . ," and so forth) was at the time vigorously debated. Men and women like Leung, KI, Elias Hagen, and Mkesne, who were instrumental in formulating and disseminating the pronouncements, were careful too not to become seen as leaders or "personalities" whose distinct characters might divert attention away from the substance of their work: they did not seek power or veneration for themselves, but only an orderly and universally conceded establishment of a different, deeper society.

(Aleila [2259–2293], obviously, has acquired a different reputation than her fellows. For many her physical and metaphysical beauty gave her a higher role than midwife to a global rebirth, and the wealth of affection directed at her from billions of people, especially after the passing of the Gaia Charter, may have contributed to her untimely end. The dispute over her character and her fate continue to this day. Valentin's *GODDESS?* [2449] is perhaps the most impartial assessment of her life and death.)

75

And what of Information?

The Declarations and the Gaia Charter were, practically speaking, only preliminary or suggested guidelines to the maintenance of the Community, intended as contracts of a sort: they were credentials of consensus, rather than marching orders. Information technology was neither outlawed nor discarded *in toto*. Now the task was simply to learn which functions of it could be replicated naturally, how the endless intertwined streets of the Community of Soul could be walked more easily than the limited avenues of artificial communication. It was not a recurrence of the Great Shame, where there had been a vast conscientious reflex away from Information, but a matter-of-fact training in a new medium. It was Aleila herself who reminded her audience in 2285 that "Anything come this far with us need not be abandoned now; seasons come and go in their time."

After all the bangs, then, came only a whimper. The last vestiges of the old ways were left standing when the new adventure began.

I have always suspected that if our economic and political problems are ever really solved, life will become simpler instead of more complex, and that the sort of pleasure one gets from finding the first primrose will loom larger than the sort of pleasure one gets from eating an ice to the tune of a Wurlitzer.

—George Orwell, "Some Thoughts
on the Common Toad," 1946

CHAPTER FIVE

Paradise Now

For all its prospects of a "pure, empathetic biosphere"—KI's words—the Community of Soul took time to grow into. Years and decades passed before it was welcomed into every home and accepted by every mind. The Gaia Charter of 2280 had ratified the initial observance of the Community by the peoples of the Earth, but it could not remake human existence all at once. The more dramatic changes at the turn of the twenty-fourth century were the long-awaited realizations of what had seemed eternal dreams: worldwide predominance of renewable energy, population stability, and general economic parity among all. Each of these were arrived at with difficulty and much dispute, over circuits traversed through many centuries. Worldwealth was in place by 2294, ZPG had been held (with minor fluctuations) since 2248, and fossil fuel consumption, even in Asia, was almost negligible by 2310. Next to such concrete, ancient-sought triumphs, the Gaia Charter felt vague and idealized.

Yet it was there nonetheless. Into the first full century of the Community of Soul the spread of thought and sentiment it expedited could be seen as an intellectual complement to newfound material comfort. Social and ecological prosperity reinforced, and were reinforced by, a gradually unfolding spiritual richness—the former were the final resolution of old conflicts, while the latter represented a Promethean departure into a novel era. How did they combine to make our present world?

First and most important was the attainment of palpable equality for every individual human being on the planet. This was not a matter of dissolving cultural distinctions or personal traits, but rather guaranteeing a day-to-day protection from hunger, violence, sickness, need, and futility. Certainly none of these wrongs had been wiped out: even now they occur here and there, and it is always possible—indeed, more possible than not—for one person to enjoy more possessions, better health, less fear, and more confidence of independent and free action than another. But what was ultimately secured by 2300 was the practical end of such discrepancies between whole land masses, between clear segments of population. "Poverty" and "plenty" became archaistic terms for extinct conditions. No more would an identifiable group of people be without what another group had in abundance. This was *The Eclipse of Pluralism* writ large, and the Declarations and the Gaia Charter made it larger still.

Environmental peace also bolstered the Community's position. The painful, painstaking healing of the natural kingdom had succeeded. The damage done by countless generations was nearly repaired. Sustainable use of resources, careful control of waste, and reproductive common sense had grown into fundamental principles of personal and collective morality. The benefit of this to a psychic society was appraised by Tanis Leung herself in her statement *The Wisdom that is Gained through Sensitivity to the Wild* (2307):

> I think intuitive contact is made more clear and more intense when *all* life is as vibrant and alive as the communicants themselves. . . . The well-being of the sky, the earth, and the seas is not only desirable for its own sake, but it also makes for an organic chorus to our conversations too. If this green Mother Earth was as blighted as it used to be in olden days, clairvoyant exchange with you all would be like searching for constellations through a dense choking haze. . . .

So the Community of Soul grew strong. Each day, everywhere, more aspects of it could be perceived, and a Golden Age of creative genius was underway: among the first great fantasies to be greeted as such were Raphella Li's harmonic trilogy *Lethe Tamed* (2311) and Ashton's *Pictures of the Ether* (2319). It was a time of incorporeal discovery, laden with wonder and opportunity, and the only blemish on the clean slate of knowledge was the continued presence of that derelict deity known as Information. In decline for three hundred years, now its terminal fall was imminent.

The overwhelming difference between pre- and post-Community reality is that now there are no barriers between thought and expression. No intermediary is required to describe the workings of one's own mind to others. Communication can be sent or received by one or many, to or from one or many, over long distances, without using an artificial agent to relay it. Much of what Information was contrived to do, therefore, can now be done as a natural ability of any conscious person.

Why, then, is it still used? What service does it still provide? There is little disagreement that at its basest, most mundane strata, Information had only muddied and demeaned and needlessly complicated conceptual transaction among women and men, but it is also admitted that at its most meaningful it had very efficiently delivered great ideas, or at any rate useful facts, to all who wanted them. *Eloquent* Information can be as stirring or as instructional to us as the ordinary thought patterns encountered every day, and for some narrow operational purposes it will likely remain a standard tool. However many its drawbacks, its handful of merits are what keeps it functioning dutifully today.

One of those merits should be conspicuous. Information can more than adequately present opinions and verities which require particular detail; it has been retained as a medium for highly technical or specialized knowledge that psychic expression cannot capture. Advanced scientific formulae, for instance, are best stored and transmitted digitally, and so is any work whose duration or linearity would not be properly transposed into the channels of the Community. Most of the traditional media are still enlisted for such tasks—virtual, aural, televisual, digital, and, in the case of books such as this one, literal.

Verbal information has neither declined nor fallen. People habitually speak to each other face-to-face as they have for millennia. But even in this there is an unmistakable subordination before the superiority of the inner tongue: language, spoken and written, has developed into a building block for the more direct instrument of straight thought. Similarly, the empirical sensations of tone, colour, texture, taste, and scent are themselves natural and undiluted, but they too are now component parts of a sublimer awareness. A rough analogy: words, symbols, and physical impressions are to the vocabulary of intuition what Latin and Greek, say, once were to the lexicon of English. They are not better or worse. They are stages in an expansion of understanding.

Yet just as Latin and Greek were not forgotten in the rise of English, so has Information continued to be acknowledged as a sort of anachronistic gateway dialect that has been distilled into a more common idiom. Historians, notably, are expected to be fluent receptors of Information, to be capable handlers of museum-piece apparatus such as phonographs and VR units, and to relate to their audiences the hieroglyphics of artificial media in natural ways. Alongside such scholarly effort, average citizens will know, by and large, that *Citizen Kane*, *The Rites of Spring*, *Descant C#*, and *Paradise Lost*, among others, are best encountered in their original formats, outside the Community of Soul. Between serious archival study and laypersons' curiosity, thus, Information keeps another dogged hold on modern pertinence.

It is the realm of Art, however, that the Community has especially recast. Whatever the majesty of a Welles, a Stravinsky, an Opus Rex or a Milton, they are sullied to us as we sense all the comparable brilliance that was never expressed or stored for posterity; "thousands of Renoirs, Beethovens, Bröntes, Kaldeks," said Somjee in 2315, "were never known, never were, could never be." Nowadays we can enjoy the limitless distribution of creativity, sharing talent unencumbered by physical restraints. Neither culture as a whole nor individual artists are dependent as they once were upon financial patronage, political license, or social climate—now it is only the raw gifts of the mind that determine the passage of lyrical visions, or humourous fancies, or sober commentaries. Critical evaluation need not be contorted by popular appeal, nor popular appeal by commercial success or failure. Li and Ashton are only the most prominent of the early fantasists: Charbajian (2296–2408), B'rema N'lan (2304–2388) and ~ (circa 2360) were less aesthetically bold, but their output, as well, was produced, conveyed, and preserved solely with the powers of thought and spirit. That basic discourse is no longer bound by synthetic syntax is a landmark in itself. Even more epochal, perhaps, is the liberation of true genius from those same impediments.

No single event or council formally demoted Information to its present rank. The nearest to a general rejection was the much-appreciated expression of 2330, Reykjavik's *BANISH WELL:*; it was also around this time that psychic precises of Gedi and La Cerra were traded widely. Worldwealth had totally assimilated the production of mechanical and digital data (and their necessary technologies) since 2309, making Information a public economic property like any other. It would never be hoarded, over- or undersold, hawked or plundered again. Other than these there were no calls to arms. There did not need to be—victory had been assured centuries before.

From 2325 onward Information finally took on the demeanour we know it by today: dully servile, old-fashioned, innocuous. Like aircraft and nuclear weapons, it survives more in principle than actuality, less actively denied than passively overlooked for other things. The intuitive masterpieces of the twenty-fourth century convinced the world that the Community of Soul was the desirable plane on which to dwell, the *lingua franca* of life, and the fabricated media it displaced assumed a plebeian, unthreatening air. Little else happened to Information. It was not dead. The civilization that surrounded it had come alive.

I met a traveller from an antique land
Who said: 'Two vast and trunkless legs of stone
Stand in the desert. Near them, on the sand,
Half sunk, a shattered visage lies, whose frown,
And wrinkled lip, and sneer of cold command,
Tell that its sculptor well those passions read
Which yet survive, stamped on these lifeless things,
The hand that mocked them and the heart that fed.
And on the pedestal these words appear—
"My name is Ozymandias, king of kings:
Look on my works, ye Mighty, and despair!"
Nothing beside remains. Round the decay
Of that colossal wreck, boundless and bare
The lone and level sands stretch far away.'

—Percy Bysshe Shelley, "Ozymandias," 1818

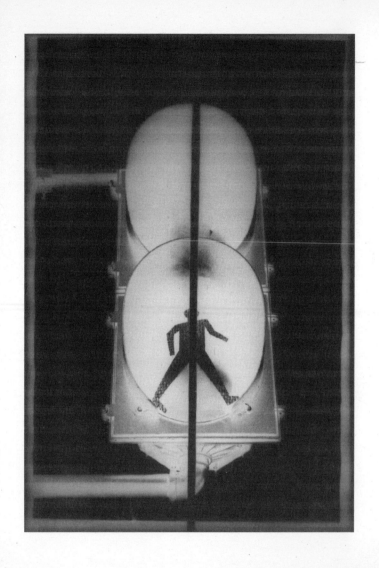

Epilogue

On June 18, 2467, Oli Soulierre addressed a gathering of several hundred people outside Tabaret Hall in Ottawa, North America. Many thousands also received her lecture around the earth. Her subject was the Information Age, examined as a historical event and explained as a human experiment—one that went sadly awry. The core of her expression has been literated here.

. . . I will define the period through three pivotal distinctions which separate it from the modern one. There are many small differences that could be cited, but I have sought to envelope them in this trio of ideas which can easily be considered and conferred between ourselves.

Firstly there is the obvious move from manufactured to organic modes of communication. During the Information Age it was supposed that the more elaborate or technically developed media were the better ones, whereas now we believe that purity and simplicity are ideal qualities of discourse. For most statements we have no reliance upon middlemen or messengers to bring them to or from each other, yet in the past the messengers dictated the substance of the message itself. The spread of knowledge, therefore, was curtailed by the very ways intended to enable it.

Second is the erasure of sectarian tailoring in favor of communal accessibility. What I mean is that when Information ruled little of it was meant to be made available to absolutely *everyone*—even "mass" or "popular" media were actually catered to precisely targeted blocs of people, divided linguistically, culturally, and so on. Often regarded as a single article, it was in fact comprised of many disparate expressions of varying aim and substance. Quality did not match quantity. *Planned obsolescence*, the deliberate incorporation of flaws or incompletions into saleable objects to ensure further trade, infested the Information industry as much as any other. Today we may choose not to take in thoughts from outside, or not to give our own thoughts away to an external public, but if we do they are all freely comprehensible. Information never was. It was "open" only in the immediate sense of being present in the routine of human life, not as something equally relevant, common or convenient to each person who encountered it.

Finally we have the basic evolution in the impetus of intelligence. For us cerebral or ethical or spiritual worth govern the diffusion of ideas, but for the people of the Information Age it was more often economic demand. Most Information was skewed toward that which could in some way or at some stage be traded for money; how much money ranged from small cash payments and regular personal remuneration to whole commercial empires and entire regional economies. We treasure the steady traffic of knowledge as its own reward. In the time of Information "knowledge" was only another means to a mercantile end. . . .

Soulierre's summary, detached and almost clinical in its observation, was one of the first occasions when "The Information Age" was depicted as having its own particular attributes, prominent figures, and major events, as a completed phase of history. It seems then a reasonable place to end our own narrative. Lacking a decisive *dénouement*, we must consider the season to have closed when an accordance of practiced erudition and general opinion is reached, however recently; not all readers will concur with our parameters of the Age, let alone its decline or fall, but we trust we have brought compelling testimony to our arguments. This version of the story, at least, is now concluded.

Was Information's regime a dark age? Not altogether. Over its course the women and men of the planet became far more *known* to one another than ever before—the phrase "global village" originated then—and far more learned in the symbiotic nature of their relationships. They reached levels of education and mental acuity that were virtually unthinkable to their predecessors. They had all the ingenuity and inspiration that had built up in the thousands of years before them to draw on. And, for good or ill, let them claim one superlative for themselves: never before or since has the human race been as *informed* as it was throughout their span. The Age of Information is aptly named.

But how slight an honour that now stands! What small triumph *merely* to be informed, to tell and be told flimsy little scraps of truth in steady, stuporous gibberish! Dazzled by and dependent upon their inventions, the citizens of Information were blind and deaf to the invisible, wordless realities in their midst. It was not just their amusements that were illusory and escapist—this they admitted to themselves—but so were their solemnities; they were equally trifling, equally marginal to permanent questions of spirit and cosmos. Not a dark age, then, yet dim and lusterless, noisy with echoes of echoes, flickered with shadows of shadows of shadows.

Was it a failure? Time does not judge this way, does not see itself as glibly right or wrong. The Information Age is better described as the gloom before the morning, as a requisite bridge into a firmer future. Its final centuries give it a taint of doom and error, but we might more charitably regard it as a natural cycle of growth and decay. The worst we could do would be to repeat its mistakes and boast of some lasting perfection, to presume ourselves and our ways to be the apex of civilization forever—as the people of the Information Age did. They thought they had achieved the crowning destiny of the world, that they had harnessed eternity. They had not. They had only begun to prepare for the coming stillness, and to withdraw themselves into the roaring, receding distance.